Alice Leaves the Palace

By: T. Grow

Readability Consensus

Based on 8 readability formulas, the text of this book has been scored:

Grade Level: 4

Reading Level: Easy to Read

Reader's age: 9-10 yrs. old

To my sister and friend, Alice Jean Kindred, you are truly a rare jewel. I am so grateful that God saw fit to order our steps in crossing paths. I want you to know that you are beautiful both inside and out, and God smiles every time I mention your name.

Once upon a time in Jewel Kingdom there lived a princess named Alice. Jewel Kingdom was the richest kingdom in the land. On every countryside you could see trees of jewels, and all the rivers and ponds flowed with treasures.

Jewel Kingdom was such a beautiful place. During the day, the gold sun shined bright and at night the pearl moon kept its remarkable glow. The evenings were always perfect for swimming, and the nights were always just cool enough to sleep with the window raised. The emerald grass throughout the kingdom provided the perfect landscape.

Alice's dad, King Johnny was a most favorable king. He was loved by all the people of his kingdom. Alice's mom, Queen Juanita was loved very much also.

The perfect parents for the perfect daughter, living in such a perfect place, only princess Alice didn't think so. She didn't know how perfect and beautiful her very own kingdom was because she never went outside. All she had was the view of the trees from her bedroom window.

Alice didn't like the way she felt when she saw herself in the mirror. So, one day she decided that she would never leave her palace again, so that no one could see how different she looked…

One evening when Queen Juanita came home, she walked in Alice's room to find her laid across her bed crying. "What's wrong sweetie? Did something happen to you?" Said the queen. "Mama, I don't want to be different anymore. Can you tell God to change me?" Alice asked.

Mama answered, "Well, why would I do that sweetie? You are my perfect little princess. I love you just the way you are." That wasn't good enough for Alice. She dropped her head and tried to convince the queen more, "But I don't look like all the other little girls in the kingdom. I just want to fit in and be like everyone else."

"Sweetie listen to me, not just with your ears but also with your heart."
Alice wasn't really sure what her mama meant by listening with her
heart, but she held her head up as the queen continued. "No, you do
not look like all the other little girls in the kingdom, but that is okay."
Alice interrupted, "It is?" "Yes, God made you the way you are because
you are special.

"Mama, are you just saying that to make me feel better?" Alice asked. The queen couldn't help but smile at Alice's concern. "Sweetie I would never tell you anything that wasn't true just to make you feel better. I want to help you understand that God does not make mistakes, and everything about you that is different in your eyes is perfect to God."

Alice was so relieved! She gave the queen the biggest hug she could squeeze out. "Thank you mama. I understand now. I want to tell God I'm sorry for not wanting to be different. Will you pray with me?" "Of course, anything for my perfect little princess", Mama said.

"God, I thank you for giving me the perfect mama and daddy to love me and take care of me. I am sorry for not wanting to be the way you have made me. Thanks for making me perfect! Amen.

Alice lifted her head with a glow on her face. She looked at the queen and smiled. "Mama, can I go outside before it gets dark?" The queen could not believe it! Her little princess wanted to leave the palace for the first time. She gladly agreed, "Of course sweetie, just don't go too far." Alice grabbed her two dolls, and rushed down the stairs and out the door.

Alice came to a pond. Playing at the edge
were two little girls. One of the little girls
spoke first. "Hello, would you like to play
with us? We are having a tea party."
Alice was thrilled! That was one of her
favorite things to do. "Sure, I have two
of my dolls with me. We can play
with them also."

The other little girl spoke. "Hi, I'm Elaine. You can be our friend now." Alice smiled, "Nice to meet you, I'm Princess Alice." The other little girl's eyes grew two sizes bigger! "Did you say princess?" Alice didn't think anything about it. "Yes, I live in the palace. What's your name?" "I'm Dominique, are you sure it is okay for you to play with us?" The little girl asked. "Of course it is. Why would you ask that?" Alice replied. "Because, we are not like you, we are different." said Elaine

Alice smiled. "That's okay, my mama said that God made me different because He wanted me to be perfect. I guess He made us all different so that we could be the perfect friends!" From that moment, the three little girls played that day and every day after...

The End

A Note from the Author

To My Little Friend,

When you look up in the sky tonight, take notice of the many stars you see. If you look really hard, you'll see that no two stars share the same twinkle. That doesn't mean that one star shines any brighter than the other one. That just means that they are different from each other. You too are a beautiful star with your own way of shinning. Just like those two stars, you may notice that there are things about you that are different from those around you. That is okay. We are all different in some ways. God gave us differences so that we all can be equally special and shine bright, just like the stars.

~T. Grow

With Love
Ms. Grow
2020

About the Author

T. Grow is a native of Prichard, AL. She moved to Huntsville, AL to attend her beloved HBCU, Alabama Agricultural & Mechanical University. After later receiving her Bachelor's Degree in Business Administration from Faulkner University, she returned to Alabama A&M University and earned a Master's Degree in Early Childhood Education in May 2017.

T. Grow is a proud mom of one son, an Elementary School Teacher, and Playwright who enjoys studying African American history.

Other Titles by T. Grow
Luci the Love Bug

www.latoyagrow.com | @authortdotgrow | ltdgrow@gmail.com

Thank you for your support!

Made in the USA
Lexington, KY
05 March 2018